GOODBYE *BINKY*

The *Binky Fairy* Story

PLUMA PRESS
NEW YORK

To Evan and Liam

When Billy was a baby, he cried a lot.
He often found it hard to fall asleep.
His mommy gave him a **Binky**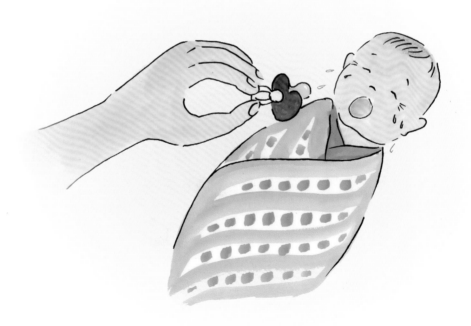
to suck on.

Billy is now two years old and is STILL sucking on his **Binky**.

He sucks it when he rides his bike...

He sucks it when he plays ball...

Sometimes he even tries to suck it when he is talking, but no one understands a word he says!

One evening as Billy's mommy tucked him into bed, she had an idea. "If it's a nice day tomorrow, let's go to the park."

When morning came, Billy woke to the sun bursting through his window.
He dressed himself as fast as he could.

Inside the park gates, Billy saw lots of boys and girls. He saw babies sitting in the shade playing in the sand; some were busily sucking on their **Binky** 🍼 pacifiers too.

Billy sat on a swing. He put his **Binky**  in his mouth and clutched both hands tightly to the long gray ropes.

Back and forth Billy soared, sucking hard on his **Binky**  so it wouldn't fall out.

He went so high he felt he could reach the clouds.

"Slow down", Billy's mommy cried out as she watched him kick his legs higher and higher towards the sky.

"Woohoooo!"

Just then, Billy's **Binky** flew out of his mouth.
"Oh no! My **Binky** ", he cried.

"Here you go," said a soft voice from behind the swing.

"I don't use a **Binky** anymore. I gave mine to Bubbles the **Binky Fairy** and now I'm a big boy".

Billy had never heard of a **Binky**  **Fairy.**
"Could the **Binky** **Fairy** make me a big
boy?" he wondered.

That night, Billy lay in his bed
busily sucking on his **Binky** .

"I want to be big",
he whispered.

Billy did not know, but those were five special words to a **Binky** 🍼 **Fairy**. Something magical was about to happen...

Suddenly, a shiny red box appeared behind Billy's bedroom door.
On one side of the box was a picture of Bubbles the **Binky Fairy** 🍼 and on the other side there appeared a magical riddle.

Put your Binky 🍼 in this box,
The choice you've made, once it's locked.
Leave it there 'till you awake,
A test it will be for you to take.
If you last till morning call,
A big boy you'll be, to one and all.

Billy wasn't sure he could fall asleep without his **Binky**. He sucked it one last time and with his mommy's help, he put his **Binky** in the red box beside his bed.

Put your binky in this box,
The choice you've made, once it's locked.
Leave it there 'till you awake,
A test it will be for you to take.
If you last till morning call,
A big boy you'll be, to one and all.

Billy tossed and turned. Left and right he wriggled and squirmed. He was finding it hard to fall asleep without his favorite blue and white **Binky** .

He closed his eyes and told himself over and over "I'm a big boy, I'm a big boy", I'm a big boy".

He finally fell asleep.

The next morning Billy couldn't believe he had slept all night without his **Binky**🍼. He suddenly felt like a VERY big boy.

Billy's **Binky** 🍼 was no longer in the shiny red box. Inside the magical **Binky** 🍼**box** was a note.

Dear Billy,

It took a lot to say goodbye to a Binky 🍼 oh so sweet,
You've made me proud by what you've done, you deserve
a special treat !

Your very special Binky 🍼 has found another home,
A baby now uses it to fall asleep alone.

So if you ever miss it, just think of this great day.
A big boy you've become. Good job to you I say.

Bubbles 🍼

The next time Billy went to the park, he smiled when he saw a baby playing in the sand sucking on a blue and white **Binky** 🍼 .

Billy wondered if that was his **Binky** 🍼 and if one day that baby would ask Bubbles the **Binky** 🍼 **Fairy** to make him a big boy too!

Visit Us on Facebook!